I0623410

SAMI

SAVE AKI MISSION I

AERIAL SUMMER

AUGUR PRESS

SAMI: SAVE AKI MISSION I

British Library Cataloguing in Publication Data.
A catalogue record for this book is available from
the British Library.

ISBN 978-1-911229-06-3

First published 2020 by
Augur Press
Delf House
52 Penicuik Road
Roslin
Midlothian EH25 9LH
United Kingdom

SAVE AKI MISSION I

Dedication

To my precious daughter and all the children of
the world.
We must not fail you.

Aerial Summer

Cover image by: Seraphina Summer

Chapter 1

Aki had lived there ever since he could remember. Since he was a baby he had had no other memories, and no other friend and home, but SAMI. He had been rocked to sleep by the deep steady movements of SAMI as he walked through what seemed to be one endless night. Walking, always walking, through deserts of darkness, through the many wastelands that had been left after the Terrible Light, until finally they had come to a place where night and day began and they were no longer under the great cloud of darkness.

SAMI was all that Aki knew, and he loved him. On SAMI's head was a clear dome, and Aki would climb up into it when he wanted to see where they were going. It was made of glass to catch the light and feed the plants and algae that grew in there.

Aki had been shown how to look after the plants by the tiny robots that had been programmed to cultivate and harvest the plants for food, which was turned into a nutritious soup that was fed into Aki by a tube. Aki had never eaten or drunk real food, so he didn't know what eating or drinking felt like. He merely knew that the tube which he would attach to SAMI when he felt empty or dry would make him feel better.

The small robots were also programmed to teach Aki ways of tending the plants so that when he grew up and they found the New Place, he would be able to grow things himself.

It was towards the New Place that SAMI strode, taking giant loping steps. He was as tall as a tower block, and inside his body were the rooms in which Aki lived. SAMI's giant silver-white robot body would glint in the sun, and it protected Aki from the harsh world outside. His legs were like giant towering tree trunks, and high up inside SAMI's dome, Aki looked very tiny. SAMI was Aki's home, his mother, his father, his best friend, his teacher… his everything.

SAMI had told Aki all about how the world was before the Terrible Light. He had shown him films of how the world had looked, and how there had been places filled with people, who all had families, homes and jobs. They made many things, and they bought and sold them from each other. Some of them did astonishingly amazing things, some of them did ordinary things that were quietly amazing – and some of those people even managed to make some of their dreams come true.

SAMI showed Aki films of great buildings, places and

incredible things that people had achieved. He also showed him films that were stories that people had imagined, and sometimes Aki would cry because in these stories people were eventually granted what they wished for most of all, and this would make him feel sad and happy all at the same time.

More than anything Aki longed to find others like himself.

Even though SAMI talked to him, Aki would sometimes feel lonely. He knew that SAMI was just a robot, and SAMI would remind him of this every now and then so that he didn't forget. Aki loved SAMI because he was all he had.

Even though SAMI was a robot, Aki could have fun with him, play games and tell jokes. And the best thing of all was a little robot that looked like Big SAMI but was all soft and furry, and Aki would sit in its arms and cuddle it whenever he felt sad. Aki sometimes felt a bit embarassed about this and didn't really want to admit to Big SAMI that it was one of his favourite things in the world.

As well as being Aki's best and only friend, SAMI made sure that Aki did his lessons for five days in a row and would then have two days off to do whatever he wanted. SAMI knew it was important that Aki was able to read and write and do his sums. Sometimes Aki found this really boring, but SAMI kept telling him that one day what he had learned would be very useful and he would realise that all the hard work had been worthwhile. SAMI always tried to keep Aki busy. He was constantly teaching him new things.

Chapter 2

It seemed as if SAMI had been walking for years, and in fact this was true. SAMI had been walking since Aki was two-and-a-half years old. Aki couldn't really remember what had happened before that – this walking was all he knew. SAMI told Aki that one day they would reach a place where the air was clean and there would be plants growing around them. He said that when they found that place Aki would be able to play outside, so he would be able to run about and go wherever he liked, instead of always having to stay inside.

Sometimes Aki felt frustrated and kicked the walls because he so desperately wanted to go outside to feel free. There were times when he felt like a prisoner, but SAMI was very firm with him. He told Aki that the air outside was poisonous and would harm him, if he went out. Sometimes Aki stopped believing that they would find the New Place. He would scream and scream until he almost made himself sick, but SAMI remained patient, and always seemed to have something helpful to say about everything. Then, when Aki had calmed down, SAMI would make him laugh and everything would be all right again. And yet sometimes Aki wondered if the 'New Place' really existed.

Since the light had come and he could see night and day, Aki loved to sit in the dome on SAMI's head, watching the landscape go past. SAMI told him the names of cities and other places as they passed them, and explained what had happened in these places. He spoke about how many people had lived there, what they had done and the ways in which they had lived. Only the shells of buildings remained, but Aki would use his imagination, to help him to picture how those cities had been. SAMI also told him about the animals and plants that had lived in the vast wildernesses that had once been teeming with life.

Aki loved to watch the sun rise and set, marvelling at this giant ball of fire in the sky, so massive and powerful, that seemed like a miracle after so many days of complete darkness. But Aki also enjoyed the night. He loved to look at the sky full of stars, which would make him think about how huge the universe must be. He would try to imagine what SAMI had told him – that each star he saw in the sky was like their own sun, or was even a distant galaxy.

He thought about how far away each sun must be for it to

look so tiny in the sky. SAMI would tell Aki the name of each constellation as it came into view, and would remind him that what they could see in the sky was only a small part of the universe, which was vast. SAMI explained that their solar system, which consisted of all the planets that moved round the sun, was part of a galaxy of stars, and that there were billions of galaxies in the universe – each billion being a thousand million. Beside this vastness, Aki was a tiny miracle of life.

SAMI said to Aki, "You are a piece of the Universe that is aware of itself – and that is a miracle." Aki asked SAMI why he wasn't also a piece of the universe that was aware of itself. To this SAMI replied that he would tell him one day, and that all Aki needed to know for now was that SAMI loved him very much and wanted only good things for him.

From time to time, SAMI had to cross rivers, streams, and sometimes even seas. On these occasions, he transformed himself into a kind of underwater boat, and it could take days or even longer to travel through wide stretches of water.

SAMI had told Aki that no creatures would have survived the Terrible Light. However, one day something slammed into the side of SAMI as they were travelling in the great sea. It banged loudly against him, and banged again. Aki felt a terrible fear unlike anything he had ever experienced before.

Quivering and shaking, he looked out of a window into the inky blackness of the sea and saw the outline of a great snake-like shape slithering around SAMI and ramming his sides. SAMI told Aki not to be afraid. He said that the creature was defending its territory, and that although it was scary, it was also a good sign because it was alive – the first living creature that they had encountered.

As they moved away from the sea creature's territory, its attacks became less frequent and eventually stopped.

After what seemed a very long time, SAMI detected land, and soon he was wading up out of the water on to a long empty beach. After pausing to do some routine maintenance because of the underwater journey, they started off again, striding into this new place. Flat land was followed by gentle hills, which soon gave way to mountains.

Chapter 3

One day, as SAMI was walking across the high mountain range, Aki felt particularly anxious because of the steep rocky faces. SAMI stopped very suddenly and Aki could hear all his processors whirring as if his sensors had picked up something new. SAMI turned his body in the direction of the west wind and opened up a sheet of fine golden gauze. Aki had only seen SAMI do this once or twice before, and he knew it meant that the air here was not so contaminated as in other places. He knew that this was a clue for SAMI, as in the past SAMI had followed the cleaner air in his search for the New Place.

SAMI seemed very excited, as many of his lights were flashing. When Aki asked him what his processors had found, he explained that it had indeed been a front of cleaner air, and that he had also detected spores.

"Spores?" said Aki. "Spores are signs of life."

"Yes," SAMI replied. "And we may discover other signs soon – seeds and plants, for example."

Aki felt a strange ache in his heart that seemed like a

mixture of excitement and happiness. SAMI had never detected spores before. Surely this must be a good sign.

Aki looked around from the mountaintop through the clear glass dome of SAMI's head. He could see for many miles. The mountains continued into the distance, and he thought that the world must be bigger than he could ever imagine, as SAMI had told him that even the view from a mountaintop was only a small part of the world – the world that had been terribly destroyed. He could see huge jagged pinnacles with snow-covered tops, steep swooping valleys and great flat plains, but everywhere was bare stone and earth, with not a hint of the beautiful green of the plants that grew in SAMI's head dome.

SAMI started to descend the mountain, following the direction of clean air in the wind. As he descended, he followed the path of a mountain stream that gradually widened and deepened. SAMI told Aki that he was following the clean air and that Aki should prepare himself.

"For what?" asked Aki.

"We may find the New Place – where you can settle, and build a home."

"Why don't you say 'we' can settle?"asked Aki.

"I will be there, but I may have to change. You will see. And there may be others."

10

"Others?" Aki repeated, astonished. He had wished that there might be others, but had never really believed that there could be. His little heart pounded with excitement and apprehensiveness. "You mean like me?" he asked.

"Perhaps, yes, like you, and you will have to learn to be friends and share everything that is there," SAMI told him.

Aki was pleased. "That's good. I would like to share."

"Even to share me?" asked SAMI.

Aki now felt confused. SAMI was his, and always had been his, so why would he have to share him?

SAMI explained that in order to live together people need to be able to share everything. Otherwise, groups of people would start to harm each other, and the world might turn to dust just as it had done before.

He told Aki that they now had a chance to make a new start. He explained that he was looking for signs of life – anything from tiny single cells to plants and perhaps even animals.

Chapter 4

As they travelled on, every so often SAMI would stop and his sensors would start to whirr. Apart from that, he was unusually quiet, and seemed to be concentrating hard. Normally Aki was his main focus of attention, but today was different. Aki was nervous, as these changes were exciting, but also a little frightening, as they were different from what he had known before.

As usual, however, SAMI walked on and on, his long steady steps forming the rhythm of Aki's life.

Then all of a sudden, as SAMI was walking over what seemed to be a vast and endless plain, he stopped. His whirring became very intense.

"What is it?" asked Aki.

SAMI did not reply, but slowly and silently bent down to examine a very small, delicate plant with a tiny white flower. It was growing out of a crack in a rock.

When Aki saw it he could hardly believe his eyes. In all his life he had never seen a living plant growing outside. He felt overwhelmed by his feelings, and wanted to cry, but instead he shouted with joy.

He knew what this meant. It meant that they might be close to the New Place, and maybe, just maybe, he would be able to go outside – and perhaps even go for a walk!

"SAMI, pick the flower so that I can see it," Aki shouted.

"No," said SAMI firmly. "We must not disturb the plant. It is the only one here, and we must let it grow and make seeds from which other plants like it can grow."

"Yes," Aki agreed. "Oh, yes."

SAMI stood up again, and his sensors surveyed the land ahead. He and Aki looked over the flat plain to the hills and the mountains beyond. The sun was setting, so Aki could no longer see clearly, but he was almost certain that they were covered in green.

SAMI seemed to know what Aki was thinking. "Perhaps tomorrow we shall see some more green," he said. Then he told Aki that now they would rest overnight, in preparation for the day ahead.

As the sun sank into darkness, SAMI's sensors continued to run quietly. Normally he would not use them, so that he could save power, but he explained that if this was the New Place, others might be coming and he needed to be ready for them.

"Why?" asked Aki. "Won't it be wonderful to see others?"

"Perhaps," SAMI replied, "but we don't know who they are – and until we do know that, we must be careful."

Aki felt anxious. He tossed and turned as he tried to get to sleep. He looked up at the familiar stars and wondered what lay ahead. SAMI rocked him steadily, and finally he drifted off to sleep, safe in the knowledge that SAMI would protect him whatever happened.

The following morning was bright and airy. It was as if the sun and the whole world around them knew that this was to be an exciting day.

Once Aki had received nutrition he looked out and saw that what he had thought he had glimpsed the day before was real. He *had* seen green hills. He could hardly believe his eyes, and his heart started to beat faster. He had never believed that this day would ever come, after everything he had seen before had been dust and emptiness.

Now, with a greater sense of purpose than ever, SAMI set off in the direction of the green hills. Even with his slow steady gigantic steps, it took him several days to reach the foot of the first slopes.

As they drew closer, Aki could see occasional clumps of low vegetation appearing on the rocky barren land. As SAMI strode on, the clumps became more and more frequent, eventually leading to an expanse of grasses of brilliant green. Then areas of bushes came into sight, and beyond them, in the distance, he could see what surely must be trees! The whole vista seemed like a miracle. Here at last, after such a long time, was this incredible oasis of burgeoning green that seemed to become ever more lush and dense as they moved further into it.

Aki marvelled at all the different types of plants, bushes and trees that he could see growing. As they travelled further into the greenness, the vegetation was taller and taller and there were more obstacles for SAMI to push through. In fact there were so many plants that his struggles almost overloaded his sensors, and for the very first time, SAMI told Aki that he must now use the controls to drive him. He explained that he needed him to do this in order to conserve his energy for processing during these additional challenges.

Aki was both shocked and excited. He had never dreamed that he would have to take over like this. Some time ago SAMI had trained Aki to drive him in a simulation, but it had never

15

entered Aki's head that he would have to do this in a real-life situation.

For a few moments Aki was not sure if he could do it, but with SAMI's gentle persuasion, he gradually took the controls of SAMI's giant body and began to pick his way carefully through the dense forest that now engulfed them.

Aki found it very strange to be in control of something so huge as SAMI, who had always been in control of everything for Aki. He found it frightening and delightful, sad and exciting, all at the same time. It was sad because somehow he felt as if he needed SAMI to be the one who did everything for him, allowing him to be like a baby sometimes, and he sensed that it meant the end of that. It was exciting because it was so thrilling to be in complete charge of everything.

Aki carefully picked his way through vines and branches, ferns, trees and bushes. He could never have believed that anything could be so beautiful. He was amazed by the endless variety of species that twirled, coiled, brushed, bent and swayed all around them, now only obstructing their progress in gentle embraces.

SAMI decided to send out a miniature drone that could fly high up to see how far this area extended and how the land lay beyond it. When Aki asked SAMI why he had never used a drone before, SAMI replied that there had never been a reason to, because previously there had been no signs of life.

The drone sent back pictures which showed that the greenness continued for many miles. SAMI explained that this was a good sign as it meant that the earth was healing itself. He also mentioned that when they reached the New Place it might be time to awaken the animals. SAMI had spoken of this before, but Aki had never really believed it. SAMI explained that one of his special holds contained the cells for many animals that had been lost from the world, and that if they found the New Place, he would need Aki's help to grow the animals from those cells and then put them back in the world. SAMI told Aki that he had the cells for one male and one female of almost every creature that had been known, so that they could start to be in the world again. Aki would have to try to make sure that they all survived.

Meanwhile the drone continued to send back pictures of how far the greenness extended, and located the very middle of it, which was where the New Place would be. As SAMI analysed the pictures, Aki noticed that there were other things – large things – moving towards the centre, too.

"SAMI" Aki exclaimed. "What are they?"

"I think that they are … the others. They are heading for

17

the same place as we are, and we shall have to meet them."

Aki was shocked by this information, and he couldn't quite believe it. "What will they be like?" he asked.

"They might be like you, or they might be different. I don't know. We must be careful, but at the same time we must show that we think rightly."

SAMI had always talked about thinking rightly. Now it seemed more important than ever to understand what he meant by this.

"What do you mean?" asked Aki.

"You know what it is to think rightly. We have spoken about this. It is when you know what is right in your heart, when you know what is good, and your weakness does not make you do something cruel in order to seem strong. And it is to understand that to be selfish can hurt others. You know that in the past people behaved like this and it was wrong, because it led to the destruction of the world. We know that we must treat nature with respect, as it is what makes our home. Too many humans were cruel and did not listen to nature. People must not make those mistakes again or they will kill themselves and everything around them."

"I'm afraid," said Aki. "I'm afraid because others are coming and I don't know what they will be like, and I won't

18

know what to do."

"It's all right to feel afraid. Being afraid is a normal feeling. But you don't need to be afraid. You will see them and you will need to be able to know clearly that the only thing to be afraid of is losing your sense of who you really are and your sense of what is right. But I know you will not lose your connection with your true self and your sense of rightness."

Aki fell silent for a while, and then asked, "Do we really have to meet them?"

"Yes," SAMI replied. "This is a part of your life, and you cannot avoid it."

Slowly Aki drove SAMI through the beautiful forest, becoming more and more confident about driving him, and revelling in being able to control the movements of his giant home and friend.

The drone guided Aki and SAMI towards a clearing at the centre of the giant forest, and they made their way there slowly and steadily.

As they drew near to the clearing, the drone took one last scan of it, and sent information to them that all the others were slowly and steadily making their way there, too. Aki wondered if all the others were as afraid as he was.

As he and SAMI moved nearer to the special place, he

could glimpse it through the trees. A beautiful golden light shone in the centre of the green forest. So this was the New Place. Aki could hardly believe that after all these years of wandering they were finally about to reach it, but he was now too apprehensive to be elated. His tiny heart was beating fast as he wondered what he would see there.

Through SAMI's audio channels Aki began to hear strange humming and buzzing sounds coming from outside. SAMI told him that these were sounds that insects were making. Staring, entranced, at the lush vegetation, Aki saw beautiful vines hanging from tree branches, and carpets of wonderful flowers of varying colours and hues. He moved SAMI onwards only very slowly, taking great care to navigate with fine-tuned skill and gentleness.

Chapter 5

As SAMI and Aki came into the clearing, giant robots appeared one by one, stopped, and stood silently.

Inside each of the huge silent robots, a small figure would come forward and look out of the glass dome at the other small figures. They seemed to be wondering, fearful, and tingling with excitement. They remained standing like this for a long time, and then one by one they inched closer to get a better view of each other. Aki noticed that each small figure was also driving its robot manually. Each small figure would look at each of the others in turn in the glass domes of their robots.

Aki looked at each robot and its occupant very carefully. Each robot looked slightly different, as did each small figure inside it. They were all children. One boy had black skin, and the other two boys had dark brown and light brown skin. There was a white-skinned girl with piercing eyes, and a pale girl with bright red hair, a brownish girl and a girl who was black-skinned like the black boy. When Aki passed her robot, she stuck her tongue out at him. He must have looked very surprised, as she collapsed into fits of giggles and lost control of her robot for a few seconds. Aki smiled and waved. She smiled and waved back, and Aki's heart soared. This was the first time he had ever had contact with another human being.

He now turned to the others and started waving frantically. He was filled with joy. The other children laughed.

Suddenly the robots switched into automatic mode and formed a circle so that they all faced each other. Intercoms that they had never used before crackled into action, and they could all hear each other breathing.

The black-skinned boy spoke first. "Do you all speak Universal?"

They all nodded. They all knew both their own language and the new language of the world, which was called Universal.

"Hi, I'm Ben," said the black-skinned boy.

"I'm Mai," said the brown-skinned girl.

"Zoya," said a girl with striking eyes.

"I'm Krishnan," said a boy with brown skin.

"I'm Ruby," said a girl with red hair.

"I'm Winna," said the black-skinned girl.

"I'm Aki," said Aki, half giggling with excitement.

"And I'm Zane," said a boy who looked a little older, and

quite tough.

"I thought I was the only one," they all said at almost exactly the same moment, and then they all laughed.

Zoya broke down and cried. She was so overwhelmed and happy to see other human beings. "I can't believe it! I can't believe it!" she cried, over and over again.

They were all so happy and so shocked that it was hard for them to know what to do or say.

"So, what are we going to do?" Ben asked. "Are we going to stand here or get out and have a look?"

There was a chorus of "Yes!" as they all agreed to get out and explore.

"Are you sure the air is clean enough?" asked Mai nervously.

"Yes," the others all chorused. "Our sensors say it is clean."

They laughed again. There would be many times from now on when they would all say the same thing or do the same thing at the same time. They had been isolated from each other, and yet they had all lived the same kind of life for such a long time.

Then Zane's robot stepped forward and Zane said, "Wait a minute. First I think we should decide who is in charge here."

"But we don't know anything about each other yet, so how can we know?" said Aki.

"That's what I mean. Someone should take charge. You can all see that I'm the oldest and I have the most experience, so it would make sense for me to be in charge."

"I don't think anyone should take charge yet. I think we have to get to know each other first, and then see how things go," Aki said.

All the others nodded in agreement.

"You're too young to understand that you need to have a leader. You don't know enough about the world, but I can help you," Zane told them firmly.

"I'm sure you know a lot of things and can be a great help, but I really think we should start off as equals and then see if we need a leader," said Aki, who was growing hot and red and experiencing feelings that he had never had before. Is this anger? he wondered. He managed to continue: "We've survived this long without a leader. I think we can survive a little longer while we work out what to do next."

"Yes," said Mai.

Ben nodded. "Absolutely. I agree."

There were mutters of agreement among the rest of the children.

Zane's face grew red. "You are trying to insult me. Why are you trying to insult me? What do you have against me?"

"Nothing. Nothing at all," said Aki quickly.

"Oh, so *you* want to be the leader," said Zane accusingly.

"No, no, not at all," Aki replied, flustered.

Zane challenged him. "Well, if you want to be the leader then we should see who is strongest and that will settle it. Come on – fight!"

"No," said Aki, "I don't want to fight you."

"You scared?"

"No," said Aki, "I just want us all to get along with each other."

"Come on, scaredy cat. Fight! Show them all who's boss!" Zane started to work the controls of his robot, then advanced it towards Aki.

"No, no, don't!" cried the other children.

Aki stared at SAMI's control panel and panicked. He didn't know what to do. He had never been in this situation before. But what about the Fight Mode button he had never used? In that split second he made his decision. He advanced SAMI towards Zane's robot, but just as they began to fight, both robots suddenly stopped and lost power.

Zane screamed and started to hit all his robot's control

panels furiously. "What is this?" he yelled. "This has never happened before. Come on, you stupid robot!"

Aki breathed a sigh of relief.

Then suddenly all the other robots failed, too. Their control panels went dead, and everything stopped.

Chapter 6

Images then began to appear in each of their consoles.

What was happening? Aki looked at the main control screen inside the console, and there he saw an image of his mother and father. They were smiling at him. He recognised them from photos that SAMI had sometimes shown to him.

And then he heard words coming from them, as if they were speaking to him.

"Hello, Aki," they said. "If you're seeing us, then you must have made it to the New Place."

Aki's mother couldn't contain her emotion and cried out, "Oh I'm so glad, my sweet love. I am so happy."

However, his father's voice was stern. "If you are watching this you will have met others and you must be operating SAMI manually. But you have asked him to fight, and SAMI will not fight here."

In these moments Aki thought that he was speaking to his parents as people, and that they were actually there, not far away from him.

"Mum, Dad," he said. "I miss you so much. I want to see you so much."

But his father continued: "The world was destroyed because people could not agree and they fought each other. Some were greedy and they refused to share what little was left. People thought that they could treat the earth as they wanted and keep taking from it without any thought or concern for its balance and well-being. Instead they destroyed much of the world and then fought over what was left. As we speak to you the end has not yet come, but we know that it will, and so we made SAMI, to save you, and that is what he must do. That's why he's called SAMI. Save Aki Mission 1. We hope you like him."

Aki smiled, and nodded, saying "I love him."

"Any differences you have with the others you must resolve by talking to each other, not by fighting," his father told him. "Millions and millions of creatures died. Please don't insult their memory by fighting."

"Mum! Dad!" Aki cried out. He wanted to hold them, but deep down he knew that he would never be able to touch them.

"Aki, we made SAMI so that you could survive. This is because we love you more than life itself. You must live and also find a way to live with others. It is our wish that you discover all the real goodness in yourself, so that you can help the world as much as possible. It is our hope that all of you who have survived find goodness within yourselves – that way you have the best chance of surviving.

"Know how much we love you. We want you to live and to be able to love as we have lived and loved, and perhaps you too will have children and then you will know even better how much we love you. SAMI was built to protect you, to look after you, and now you will have to say goodbye to him as he was, so that you can build a new life here. You will have to take him apart. You will find that he is built so that you can make him into a home, farm buildings and a tractor with a plough, and we hope that this will be enough to get you started."

"But I can't take him apart! I love him. He's all I've got!"

Aki's mother looked at him sympathetically through the console. "We know it will be hard for you, but you must start again. You are ready. You have taken the controls for yourself. You will still have the things that will come from the parts of SAMI's body, and you will have Little SAMI to hold close. Everything that Big SAMI has been for you will be with you, just in a different way." His mother faltered before continuing. "It will be just as we are with you, in the wind and

29

the earth and our love for you which goes beyond time."

Aki felt that he was choking. He could hardly bear what was happening.

"Mum …"

"Now, Aki, go and meet your new friends. I'm sure you will make wonderful friends among these boys and girls."

"Mum!"

Tears started to pour down Aki's face.

Aki's father smiled. "Go on – go and be with them. And remember your manners."

Before Aki could answer, his mother blew him a kiss and the images on the screen faded out.

"Don't go!" he cried.

He stood staring at the screen. He clutched at his chest and whispered "I love you."

Aki shook his head. His heart ached but somehow he was also able to feel joy about the friendships he had yet to make. He asked SAMI if he could now go out and meet the others. SAMI told him that he must do this, and that he should not be afraid. He reassured Aki that he trusted that he had learned wisdom and had a good heart, and that this meant he would know what to do.

Aki's heart was beating fast as he took the lift down

SAMI's leg to the ground – a journey he had never made before. There he waited for SAMI's final checks of the air and the surroundings, before the door could slide open.

SAMI beeped an 'All Clear', and slowly the door to the world opened. For the first time in his life Aki felt the soft breath of warm wind on his face. He closed his eyes in order to savour it. It was like nothing he had ever felt before. Somehow he knew that this gentle wind was part of the great wind of the whole planet, the breath of the earth. It was exquisite. And the fragrant scent of life came with it.

He opened his eyes and took a step out into the world. It was so strange not to be surrounded by the huge protecting shape of SAMI, and he suddenly felt very vulnerable. He wondered how he was supposed to feel strong when he was so tiny.

One by one all the children emerged from the giant robots that had carried them there. Some ran and whooped, while others stood and stared around them in awe. But one child was missing.

Aki walked over to Zane's robot and looked up. Zane was no longer at the control panel. Aki tried the door, and slowly it opened to reveal that he was slumped on the floor, sobbing, and gasping for breath.

Zane had remembered his parents and he was hurting very badly. He hurt so badly that he needed to share the pain, but he had no way to express it except by wanting to fight. Aki began to realise that pain could sometimes have this effect. He took Zane in his arms and held him. Everyone there would have their own pain. They were all going to have to work out how to live with it, and do their best to help each other.

Aki helped Zane up. Zane looked at Aki and said "sorry" quietly and meaningfully. Aki smiled, nodded and said, "That's behind us. Let's go together and take a look around."

They walked out into this new fragrant green world that was brimming with wonderful new sounds and bursting with colour, light and fragrance. They had always seen the world from behind a sheet of glass and now it seemed so different, so alive. They saw tiny insects in between the leaves, flowers emerging from plants, and berries forming. It all seemed impossibly beautiful compared with the barren world that they had seen for so many years. Each of them would shake the giant palm leaves and let droplets of water cascade down on them, and they would laugh with pure joy.

Sometimes they would just sit and stare at each other, and then reach out and touch each other's skin in disbelief. The feel of another person's skin was so beautiful, so precious, that they found it hard to understand how the previous world had come to an end.

When darkness fell they made their first fire and gathered round it, looking up at the vast star-filled sky, and for the first time they sat with others like themselves and talked and laughed well into the night.

Chapter 7

The next morning was cold and wet, and they began to be aware of the reality of what lay ahead of them. Each child went to their robot and activated the programs for the New Place. Aki was excited as he told SAMI about everything that he had experienced. He chattered and laughed, and SAMI responded in his usual way – with patience, interest and, as always, with logic. Aki now understood the difference between speaking to another human being and talking to a robot. It was difficult to say exactly what it was, but other humans interrupted, laughed, said silly things and pulled faces – none of which SAMI could do. But Aki still loved SAMI very much.

SAMI said he was happy that Aki had made friends, and that now it was time to disassemble his robot body to build the objects that he would need in his new life.

"Disassemble?" said Aki. "No! Not yet!"

"You already know that I am built so that I can be taken apart and used as equipment and tools. I am made up of parts for a tractor that you will need to farm, and parts to enable you to build a house. And you will see that the other robots also have practical uses."

"No!" cried Aki. "No, I can't do that. I can't lose you. I won't do it!" He began to cry. The thought of losing SAMI was too much for him to bear.

"I will always be with you, Aki, but just in a different form. I will be all around you in your new home and in the things you use. I will be there in the way that the plants grow and in the food that you eat. Your parents are in me. They will always be with you, too. And, of course, you will always have your Little SAMI."

At this point, Little SAMI walked up to Aki and gave him a hug. His small face even formed a smile for him. This made Aki laugh, and he could see that even though it broke his heart to lose the Big SAMI that he had always known, he knew what SAMI was telling him was right.

"Let's just enjoy all the changes," SAMI said to him.

This was the most human thing that SAMI had ever said. Aki wondered if SAMI had become more like him, even though he had always maintained he was not the same as a human.

When all the children talked again they found that they

were all equally shocked that they had to take apart their precious robots, but they found that speaking to each other about this somehow made it seem less bad.

Zane said that his robot had parts for a flying machine. Aki told his friends that SAMI had storage towers for grain, components for a tractor, and sections for a house. Zoya's robot had parts for a windmill, a greenhouse and a water distiller. At first, Ben struggled to understand some of what was stored inside his robot, but then he worked out that there were hand tools he needed to work with metal and wood. He remembered seeing some like this in pictures that his robot had shown him of life as it had been. He also had a large shed, a windmill and a water pump. Mai had a science lab. Winna had a truck, a hospital and medicines. Krishnan had a library containing many old books and art works, and computers and printers of many different kinds. Ruby had a rocket.

They soon began to realise that together they could build a future.

Slowly, one day at a time, they began to take their robots apart and build all the things that they needed for that future.

SAMI was still there as Aki's tractor and home, and Little SAMI went everywhere with Aki.

They took all the animal cells and used the male and female ones to make embryos, which they grew very carefully in Winna's science lab. When the embryos had grown into baby animals, they then had to nurture them and look after them as they matured. Each of the animals was extremely precious, as no others existed apart from them.

Aki sowed his first seeds, and the harvest ripened just as the first of the baby animals had become fully formed. Cattle, sheep and goats were developing. Bird eggs hatched. And there were many more creatures to come.

When they had grown their first crop, the children sat down together to taste food for the first time. They took the strawberries, carrots and peas which had been the first crops that they had harvested. They all looked at each other with trepidation. They had been taking in nutrients and water through tubes attached to their homes, but now this real food was available. Each child reached for the fruit and placed it in their mouth for the first time. Aki put a strawberry in his mouth and his eyes widened. At first the fruit created a strange sensation, but then a wild sweet taste spread through his mouth and gave him a sensation of goodness that he could only express with a very wide smile. Each child tried a different food, and squeals, sighs and laughs of excitement and delight burst from them as they tasted each new flavour. Chewing meant that their jaws moved in new ways.

Aki looked about him at the new world they were creating, and he wondered how people could have destroyed anything so incredible, so beautiful and so precious.

SAMI had always said, 'The good you seek is in yourself.' And Aki knew that they would need to find all the good in themselves if they were to start the world anew and prevent what had happened before from ever happening again.

Cover design: Martin Pullinger

www.ingramcontent.com/pod-product-compliance
Lightning Source LLC
Chambersburg PA
CBHW032113170626
46808CB00008B/3049